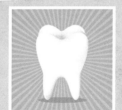

# Letters from My Tooth Fairy

by Betsy Cramer

DORRANCE
PUBLISHING CO
EST. 1920
PITTSBURGH, PENNSYLVANIA 15238

Dorrance Publishing Co
585 Alpha Drive
Pittsburgh, PA 15238
Visit our website at www.dorrancebookstore.com

ISBN: 978-1-6393-7281-2
eISBN: 978-1-6393-7681-0

To my three granddaughters

Hi, my name is ZeZe. I LOVE kindergarten, especially recess playing on the jungle gym. Since school started I have been Superstar five times! That means I follow the rules. School started two weeks ago, I think. I also love my 'aminals'. I have one dog; named Pickles because she used to eat dill pickles when she was a puppy, eleven fish (mostly Neon Tetras), one frog named Hoppy, and seven chickens who we named after Snow White's Seven Dwarfs.

I have had my first loose tooth loose for months. My friend, Tomas, tried to scare it out with a big loud BOO! My dad said he would tie a string around the tooth and the bathroom doorknob and slam the door shut. I THINK he was teasing. Mom suggested she tickle it out. She loves to tickle. Even my dog, Pickles, tried to trip me so I'd fall on my face. No luck. At school kids in my kindergarten class go around wiggling their teeth in front of me. They bring their special tooth fairy boxes for Show and Tell.

Yesterday I ran home from school yelling, "Mom! I ran straight into the back of Tomas's head and my loose tooth fell out."

"Oh no! Did you lose it?"

"No, but I stepped on it."

"Oh dear, honey, let's see. It's STILL a perfectly pearly white tooth for the tooth fairy."

When I went to bed that night I told Mom, "I want to stay awake all night and talk to the tooth fairy."

Mom looked at me and smiled, "Well, just in case you DO fall asleep, let's write a letter and put your beautiful tooth in the tooth box Grandma gave you."

So we wrote, actually Mom wrote:

*Dear Tooth Fairy,*

*I bumped into Tomas and my wiggly loose tooth flew out. Hope you know where to find me.*

*Love ZeZe*


I laid back on my pillow, eyes wide open and waited for the tooth fairy.

"Where is she?" I wondered. "When will she get here?" I thought with my fingers wrapped tightly around my tooth fairy box.

The next morning I jumped out of bed.

"Mom, Mom! I got a $2 dollar bill under my pillow AND a letter."

Mom read the letter:


*Dear ZeZe,*

*Thank you for your beautiful "pearly white." You took good care of it. Everyone in the Fairy Forest thanks you.*

*Your Tooth Fairy, Celeste*

The next day I took my letter to school to show Tomas, who was already upside down on the jungle gym.

"Doesn't she have a wonderful name? My dad says Celeste means sky." I said joining him also upside down.

"I wonder if the Fairy Forest is up in the sky?" he asked very interested. Tomas is playing "space commander." The inside of the jungle gym is his mission control. He wants me to ask the tooth fairy just where the Fairy Forest is.

"Maybe we can travel in my rocket for a visit. Ask her next time you lose a tooth." He laughed.

Now in school we're learning to count to one hundred. I haven't lost a tooth in months. But I do have a wiggly one. Tomas chases me around the playground hoping I will bump into him again. But in class, my tooth just fell out right into my hand. I was sitting on my mat reading *Vivian Loses a Tooth*. I was excited and ran to Ms. Robertson, my teacher. She gave me a little green plastic monkey case

to put it in so I wouldn't lose it in my backpack and a wet paper towel to put in the tooth hole.

When I got home I explained to Mom, "Nobody did anything. It just fell out. I've got to write a note to Celeste right away."

Mom got out the note paper with kittens in a basket on it. "Well, what do you want to say?"

*Dear Celeste, My Tooth Fairy,*

  *Do you live with a lot of other tooth fairies? I hope you like my new "pearly white."*

  *Love, ZeZe*

I tucked the envelope with the tooth and card under my pillow and waited and waited and waited to meet Celeste. This time I was determined to stay awake. I decided to try counting to one hundred.

The next morning I was so sad. I fell asleep! But there was something scratchy tickling my ear. Another note *AND* another $2 dollar bill. I ran to the kitchen where Mom was making pancakes.

"Mom, can you read my note from Celeste?"

"Of course," she said as she flipped a Mickey Mouse pancake over carefully. "It says,"

*Dear ZeZe,*

*Your "pearly white" is wonderful. I will be proud to give it away.*

*I don't live in the sky. I live in a ferny, feathery, fairy forest. I have lots of friends who live here too. We make our beds in nests high in the branches of an acacia tree. We eat nectar from all the beautiful flowers around us. It is always warm and safe. Say hi to Tomas.*

*Love, Celeste, Your Tooth Fairy*

I showed Tomas my letter the next day at recess. It was cold and rainy outside, which meant indoor recess. Everyone was drawing and playing at their desks. Tomas began drawing a picture of him flying his rocket into the Fairy Forest. I was drawing a picture of Celeste in her nest in the Fairy Forest while whistling through the hole made where my new teeth will be.

It is Memorial Day today. School is almost out for the summer. I have another VERY loose tooth that I keep pushing my tongue against. My fingers like to wiggle it. And when I bite on the apple in my lunch, I can't help yelling, "Ow!"

That night, while eating yummy cheese pizza with my family, I suddenly coughed and let out a cry. "I swallowed it!" I gagged, opening my mouth to show the gaping hole on the bottom where my tooth used to be. Pickles woofed, hoping some pizza had fallen to the floor for her. Dad looked surprised and started to laugh. Mom ran to my side to comfort me. I started to cry. I was worried

the tooth fairy wouldn't visit me. "You have to h…h…have a tooth," I sobbed.

At bedtime I was sad. I had no tooth to give to Celeste. I would get no $2 dollar bill or letter.

Mom said, "Write a letter anyway. Maybe the tooth fairy knows you lost your tooth"

So, on puppy note paper this time Mom wrote a very short note for me:

*Dear Celeste, My Tooth Fairy,*
*I ATE MY TOOTH! I'm sorry.*
*Love, ZeZe*

When I woke up the next morning, I slowly and cautiously checked under the pillow. There was  a present and a note. This time I ran to Dad, who was eating breakfast and reading the paper.

"She gave me a $2 dollar bill and a letter! I don't think she's mad," I said excitedly. Together we opened the note.

*Dear ZeZe,*

*So sorry you ate your beautiful "pearly white"! That happens sometimes. Still you take very good care of all your teeth and I know I will get more soon. Be good.*

*Love from Your Tooth Fairy, Celeste*

When I showed the note to Tomas he was happy for me.

"I wonder what the tooth fairy does with all the teeth? Next time ask her."

In early summer just after school ended, my family went camping with my cousin, Carmen and her family. Camping was so fun. We climbed trees, played on the lake beach building sand castles, swam underwater in the lake looking for crabs, and jumped up and down on the air mattress in the tent. We both had loose teeth. Carmen's was way wigglier. Actually, I had two slightly loose front teeth.

One afternoon, we were jumping along a horizontal tree trunk bouncing it up and down. It was like a balance beam. Carmen is very good on the balance beam. Suddenly we both let out a loud shriek. We had bounced off the swaying tree and fallen with a crash onto the stony ground below. I lost BOTH front teeth! Carmen's was still dangling in place. We started to bawl and our parents came running. Our moms were cradling us and, in panicked voices, asking what happened. My dad was holding Kleenex in my bleeding mouth while Uncle Mike was searching the ground for my teeth. It turned out my teeth were WAY more ready to come out and they were not broken. Everyone had calmed down. Pickles licked the tears from my face and rolled over for a belly scratch.

Mom helped me write the letter to Celeste in the tent that night. I remembered that Celeste lived in a forest like the one Carmen and I were camping in.

*Dear Celeste, My Tooth Fairy,*

*I think you must live in a beautiful place. I picture you eating flower cakes at sunset and swinging in your nest as you sleep. Carmen and I are camping in a pine and oak forest. It smells wonderful. We actually fell off a tree branch and both my front teeth popped out. I'm alright, but do you know where we are?*

*What do you do with all the teeth you take from kids? Tomas wants to know and I guess I do too. Hope you find me.*

*Love, ZeZe*

*P.S. Mom says I will never be able to stay awake all night. I say I will.*

Next morning, Mom is frying bacon on the outdoor cook stove, while Dad and Uncle Mike are baking biscuits in a Dutch oven over the camp-fire. Auntie Alex is fixing the fluffiest scrambled eggs on earth. Breakfast around a camp table is always delicious

I brought my $2 bill and the note to the table very happy the tooth fairy found me.

Carmen came to the table excitedly and said, "I lost my tooth this morning. Yipee! "She shows everyone the tiny tooth happily. Everyone claps or says, "Good job."

Then Carmen asked, "How about you ZeZe? Did the tooth fairy find you?"

"Yes," I said excitedly. I shoved the letter into Mom's hand to read.

*Dear ZeZe,*

*Two "pearly whites"! Thank you, thank you. I'm sorry you fell out of a tree, but happy you are having a good time camping. I love my ferny, feathery forest. I love flying through the trees and sometimes I bump into one of my friends.*

*My fairy friends and I collect your teeth to give tiny, "pearly white" teeth to all the babies of the world. Baby teeth just stay in for a little while, so it's like recycling. If you got those big teeth when you were a baby you sure would look* really *funny. Meanwhile, you practice keeping your teeth clean and "pearly white" for when you get your big teeth. Keep up the good brushing! Say hello to Carmen.*

*Love, Your Tooth Fairy Celeste.*

Carmen ran to her tent to get flowery note paper. She was ready to write her letter to the tooth fairy. She was happy that the tooth fairy knew where they were.

"What would her tooth fairy's name be? Did she live with Celeste?" She lay on her pillow, eyes wide open waiting for HER tooth fairy.